The Best Vest Quest

Written by Alice Hemming

Illustrated by Alex Paterson

Collins

King Chester's vest had a rip and a food splash.

I am on a quest
for a better vest!

King Chester got a metal vest.

This vest is too hard! The Best Vest must be soft.

The next vest was as soft as a kitten.

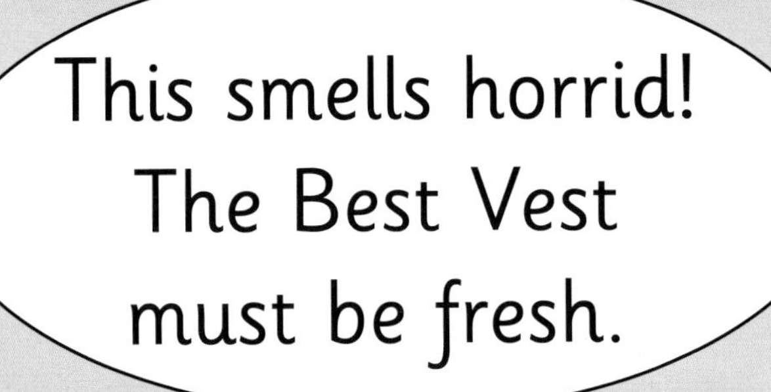
This smells horrid!
The Best Vest
must be fresh.

Then King Chester got a tight pink vest.

This smells good, but it is far too little!

In the end, King Chester went back to **his** soft, snug vest.

I can mend it
and scrub it!

The quest had ended.

My vest is best of all!

The best vest

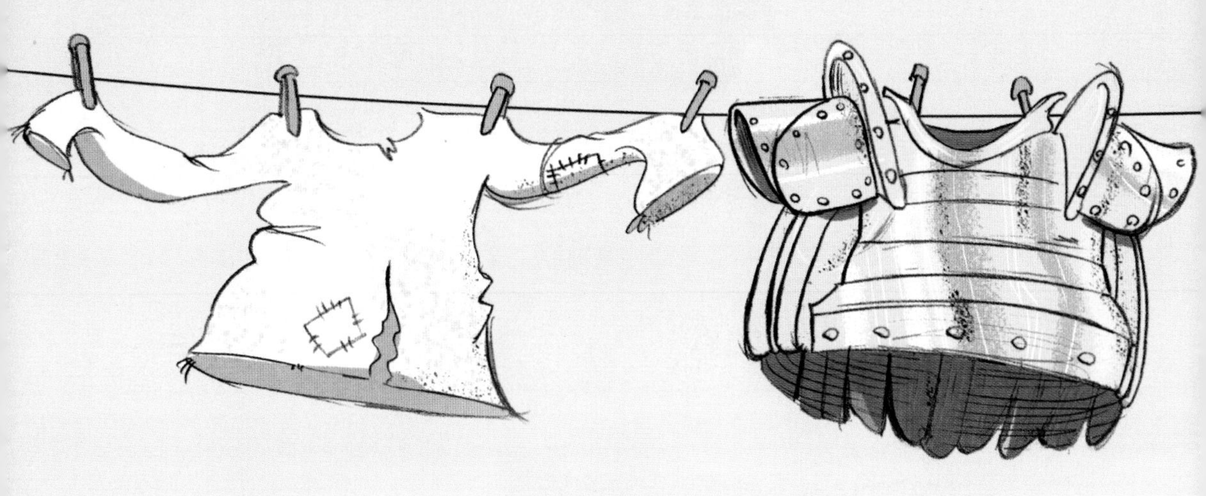

After reading

Letters and Sounds: Phase 4

Word count: 100

Focus on adjacent consonants with short vowel phonemes, e.g. /v/ /e/ /s/ /t/

Common exception words: of, to, the, I, all, my, was, be, little

Curriculum links (EYFS): Understanding the World: People and Communities

Curriculum links (National Curriculum, Year 1): Geography: Human and Physical Geography

Early learning goals: Listening and attention: children listen to stories, accurately anticipating key events and respond to what they hear with relevant comments, questions or actions; Understanding: answer 'how' and 'why' questions about their experiences and in response to stories or events; Reading: read and understand simple sentences, use phonic knowledge to decode regular words and read them aloud accurately, read some common irregular words

National Curriculum learning objectives: Spoken language: listen and respond appropriately to adults and their peers; Reading/word reading: apply phonic knowledge and skills as the route to decode words, read aloud accurately books that are consistent with their developing phonic knowledge and that do not require them to use other strategies to work out words; Reading/comprehension: develop pleasure in reading, motivation to read, vocabulary and understanding by being encouraged to link what they read or hear read to their own experiences

Developing fluency

- Your child may enjoy hearing you read the book.
- You may wish to read alternate pages, encouraging your child to read with expression.

Phonic practice

- Practise reading words that contain adjacent consonants. Model sounding out the following word, saying each of the sounds quickly and clearly. Then blend the sounds together.

  s/o/f/t
- Ask your child to say each of the sounds in the following words. Now ask them to blend the sounds together.

  s/n/u/g   m/e/n/d   v/e/s/t   s/c/r/u/b
- Now ask your child if they can read each of the words without sounding them out.